CINDERELLA

The Graphic Novel

retold by Beth Bracken   illustrated by Jeffrey Stewart Timmins

STONE ARCH BOOKS
www.stonearchbooks.com

Graphic Spin is published by Stone Arch Books
151 Good Counsel Drive, P.O. Box 669
Mankato, Minnesota 56002
www.stonearchbooks.com

Library of Congress Cataloging-in-Publication Data
Bracken, Beth.
 Cinderella: The Graphic Novel / retold by Beth Bracken; illustrated by Jeffrey Stewart Timmins.
 p. cm. — (Graphic Spin)
 ISBN 978-1-4342-0764-7 (library binding)
 ISBN 978-1-4342-0860-6 (pbk.)
 1. Graphic novels. [1. Graphic novels.] I. Timmins, Jeffrey Stewart, ill. II. Cinderella. English.
III. Title.
PZ7.7.B73Cin 2009
[Fic]—dc22
                                                             2008006720

Summary: Cinderella's wicked stepmother won't let her go to the ball. But with a little help from a
Fairy Godmother, she'll be getting there in style. There's just one catch. At midnight, her magical
gown will turn back into dirty old rags.

Art Director: Heather Kindseth
Graphic Designer: Kay Fraser

Librarian Reviewer
Julie Potvin Kirchner
Educator, Wayzata Public Schools
BA in Elementary Education, The College of Saint Catherine, Saint Paul, MN
MA in Education, The College of Saint Catherine, Saint Paul, MN
MLS, Texas Woman's University

Reading Consultant
Elizabeth Stedem
Educator/Consultant, Colorado Springs, CO
MA in Elementary Education, University of Denver, CO

1 2 3 4 5 6 13 12 11 10 09 08

Printed in the United States of America

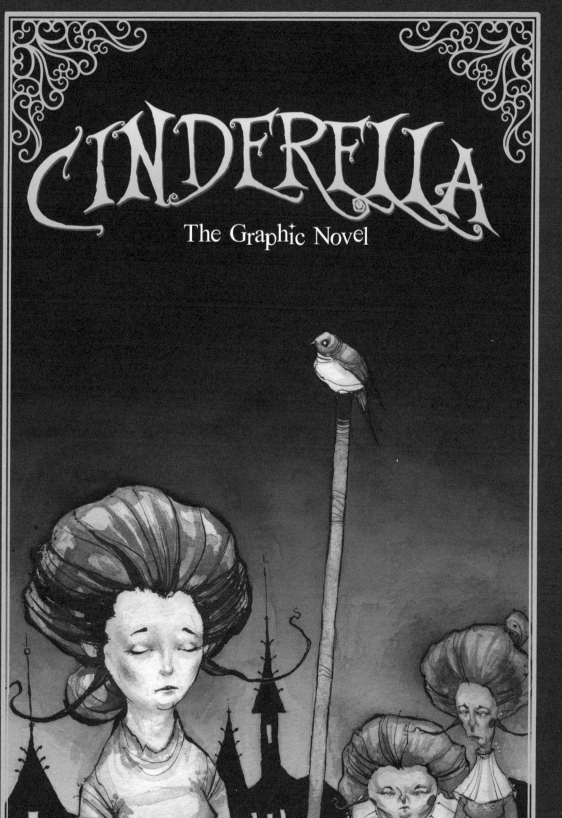

CINDERELLA

The Graphic Novel

CAST OF CHARACTERS

THE EVIL
STEPMOTHER

THE EVIL
STEPSISTERS

THE FAIRY
GODMOTHER

THE PRINCE

THE FATHER

CINDERELLA

Every day, she went to her mother's grave and wept.

Winter came, and the snow spread a white sheet over the grave, but Ella's sadness continued.

By early spring, Ella's father had found another wife.

Cinderella planted the twig on her mother's grave. She cried so much that her tears fell on the twig and watered it.

Soon, the twig became a handsome tree, budding with leaves and home to many kind birds.

Still, it could not cure Cinderella's sadness.

Then one day, a messenger arrived at the house . . .

Hear ye! Hear ye! The king has issued a proclamation!

A ball in his son's honor will take place in three days.

Every young woman is invited, and the prince will choose a bride!

Oh, my!

Did you hear that girls? You better find something to wear.

I will wear my red velvet dress with French lace trimming!

And I will wear my gold flowered cloak and my diamond necklace!

POOF!

Oh, my! It's wonderful!

Yes, but there's still a few things missing.

And a couple of these little creatures will be very useful for you!

POOF!!

23

Cinderella and the prince danced for hours.

What a lovely princess!

If you were more like her, you might get the prince's attention!

They danced so long, in fact, that Cinderella forgot what her godmother had said.

Suddenly . . .

GONG!

GONG!

GONG!

Oh, no! I lost track of time! I have to go!

But why?!

Cinderella didn't answer him, and by the time he got out of the castle . . .

GONG! GONG! GONG!

Cinderella was gone.

GONG! GONG! GONG!

But she had left something behind.

A few days later . . .

Hear ye, hear ye! To find his mysterious maiden, the prince will try her slipper on every woman in the kingdom!

If the slipper fits a maiden, he will marry her!

Oooh!

Soon, the prince brought the slipper to Cinderella's house.

Do any maidens live here?

Just my two daughters, your highness. But one of them is surely your mystery princess.

29

ABOUT THE AUTHOR

Beth Bracken is a children's book editor. She lives in St. Paul, Minnesota, with her husband, Steve, and their dog, Harry, a Jack Russell terrier who thinks he's a lion. When she's not reading, writing, or editing books, Beth spends most of her time knitting endlessly while watching reruns of old TV shows and drinking lots of tea.

ABOUT THE ILLUSTRATOR

Jeffrey Stewart Timmins was born July 2, 1979. In 2003, he graduated from the Classical Animation program at Sheridan College in Oakville, Ontario. He currently works as a freelance designer and animator. Even as an adult, Timmins still holds onto a few important items from his childhood, such as his rubber boots, cape, and lenseless sunglasses.

GLOSSARY

ashamed (uh-SHAMED)—felt embarrassed and guilty

ball (BAWL)—a formal party where people dance and interact

cinders (SIN-durz)—small pieces of wood or coal that have been partly burned

disgusting (diss-GUST-ting)—very unpleasant to others

godmother (GOD-muhth-ur)—a woman who protects a child beginning at birth

hearth (HARTH)—the area in front of a fireplace

highness (HYE-ness)—a title given to members of a royal family

madam (MAD-uhm)—a formal title for a woman

messenger (MESS-uhn-jur)—someone who delivers messages

miserable (MIZ-ur-uh-buhl)—sad or unhappy

proclamation (prok-luh-MAY-shuhn)—a public announcement

turtledoves (TUR-tuhl-duhvz)—small, wild, friendly birds

vile (VILE)—evil or immoral

THE HISTORY OF CINDERELLA

The story of Cinderella has been told for hundreds of years in more than a thousand different ways. In fact, the earliest known version dates back to about A.D. 860. That's more than 1,100 years old! It appeared in a Chinese book of legends called *Miscellaneous Morsel from Youyang*. The author, Tuan Ch'eng-Shih, titled the story "Ye Xian." Although the title was different, many parts were the same as today's versions of Cinderella, including the evil stepmother and a pair of golden slippers.

For many years after, people told the tale of Cinderella. They passed the story orally from person to person, meaning it was never written down. In 1634, Italian Giambattista Basile finally recorded the tale again for his book *The Tale of Tales, or Entertainment for Little Ones*. Many believe Basile's book inspired some of the most popular versions of Cinderella.

In 1697, Frenchman Charles Perrault based his version off of Basile's work. However, Perrault also added his own twist on the tale. He introduced a fairy godmother, and he added a pumpkin carriage and a few animal servants. He also made the famous slippers glass instead of gold.

In the early 1800s, brothers Jacob and Wilhelm Grimm, two famous fairy tale writers, created yet another version. They called the story "Aschenputtel," or "Ash Girl." In their tale, the stepsisters are punished for being mean to Cinderella. At the end, the sisters' eyes are pecked out by doves!

Of the many versions, however, Disney's Cinderella remains one of the most famous. Released in theaters on February 15, 1950, Cinderella quickly became one of the highest-grossing films of the year. It has inspired even more versions of this famous tale.

DISCUSSION QUESTIONS

1. Why didn't the prince care that Cinderella was dusty and dirty?
   What does his reaction tell you about his character?

2. Each page of a graphic novel has several illustrations called
   panels. What is your favorite panel in this book? Describe what
   you like about the illustration and why it's your favorite.

3. Fairy tales are often told over and over again. Have you heard
   the Cinderella fairy tale before? How is this version of the story
   different from other versions you've heard, seen, or read?

WRITING PROMPTS

1. Fairy tales are fantasy stories, often about wizards, goblins, giants, and fairies. Many fairy tales have a happy ending. Write your own fairy tale. Then, read it to a friend or family member.

2. Pretend you have a fairy godmother that could grant you three wishes. What three things would you ask for and why?

3. Write your own version of Cinderella using people you know as the characters. Who will be the fairy godmother? Who will be the evil stepsisters? You can even make yourself a character!

INTERNET SITES

The book may be over, but the adventure is just beginning.

Do you want to read more about the subjects or ideas in this book? Want to play cool games or watch videos about the authors who write these books? Then go to FactHound. At *www.facthound.com*, you'll be able to do all that, and more. The FactHound website can also send you to other safe Internet sites.

CHECK IT OUT